CRABBY CRATCHITT

by GREGORY MAGUIRE

illustrated by ANDREW GLASS

CLARION BOOKS NEW YORK

To Nina Ignatowicz—G.M.

For Millie, my dear old friend—A.G.

Clarion Books
a Houghton Mifflin Company imprint, 215 Park Avenue South, New York, NY 10003

The illustrations for this book were executed in watercolor pencils and oil crayons. The type was set in 16-point Opti Adrift.

Printed in Hong Kong

Library of Congress Cataloging-in-Publication Data
Maguire, Gregory.
Crabby Cratchitt / by Gregory Maguire; illustrated by Andrew Glass.
p. cm. Summary: Crabby Cratchitt has a hen whose constant clucking is so annoying, Crabby devises
a plan to cook her in a frying pan. ISBN 0-395-60485-0 [1. Chickens Fiction. 2. Farm life Fiction.
3. Stories in rhyme.] I. Glass, Andrew, ill. Title.
PZ8.3.M273Cr. 2000 [E]—dc21 99-41094
CIP
SCP 10 9 8 7 6 5 4 3 2 1

Crabby Cratchitt had a farm,
E-I-E-I-oh.
And on that farm she had a hen,
E-I-E-I-oh.

With a cluck cluck here

and a cluck cluck there.

Too much clucking everywhere.

Here a cluck,

there a cluck,

sounded like a record stuck.

At naptime Crabby liked to rest.
But then the hen would cluck with zest.

E-I-E-I-no!

Crabby didn't like her hen—
all that noise, and noise again.
The hen was lonely, so she stayed
near to Crabby, never strayed.
Crabby cried, "You loudmouth! Shoo!
I need my nap! I'm warning you!"
What could Crabby Cratchitt do?
If you were Crabby, what would *you*?

Crabby had a clever plan.
She'd cook that hen in a frying pan!
E-I-E-I-yum yum yum.

cluck!

Crabby Cratchitt had a hatchet,
E-I-E-I-oh.
To cook a bird, you have to catch it,
E-I-E-I-oh.
Crabby Cratchitt raised the latch
to let the hen go out to scratch.
Crabby knew that hens can't fly.
Crabby held the hatchet high.
Crabby tripped upon a bump.
Crabby learned that hens can jump.
The hatchet struck a nearby stump,
E-I-E-I-my oh my.

Crabby Cratchitt had a net,
E-I-E-I-oh.
She'd get that noisy chicken yet,
E-I-E-I-oh.
The trap caught Crabby for an hour
in a sudden summer shower.
Crabby struggled to get free.
Keeping Crabby company,
the hen decided to perform
on and on, throughout the storm.
E-I-E-I-mi-mi-mi!

cluck
cluck
cluck
cluck
cluck

Crabby Cratchitt, at it still.
That hen was pretty hard to kill.
In the cornfield Crabby saw
a funny scarecrow made of straw.
A light went on in Crabby's eyes.
She'd scare the hen with a great disguise.
Dressed in the scarecrow's floppy hat,
Crabby terrified the cat.
But the hen was full of pluck.
She jumped up top with a cluck, cluck, cluck.

cluck
cluck
cluck

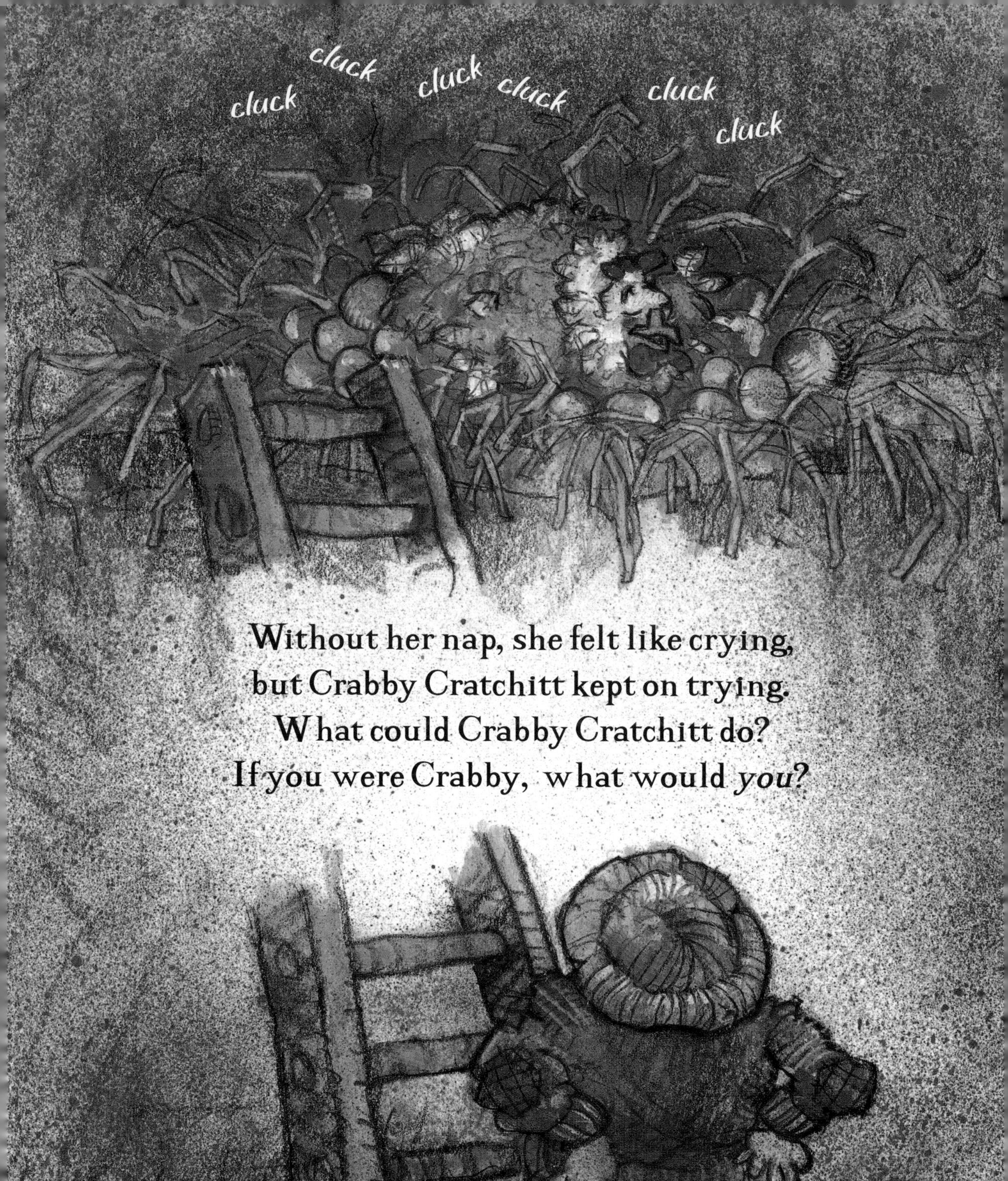

Without her nap, she felt like crying,
but Crabby Cratchitt kept on trying.
What could Crabby Cratchitt do?
If you were Crabby, what would *you*?

The hen went clucking as before,
and laid two dozen eggs or more.
Then she heard Crabby Cratchit say,
"I have to cart those eggs away!
If they should hatch and chirp and cheep,
I'd never *ever* get to sleep!"

Crabby Cratchitt had a plan,
E-I-E-I-oh.
"I'll sell the eggs to the grocery man!"
E-I-E-I-oh.

The hen went clucking in alarm,
to think her eggs might come to harm.
But Crabby wouldn't change her mind.
Every egg that she could find
she packed inside a wooden box.
And who was hiding near?

A fox!

The hen stood like a hen of stone,
silent, sad, and all alone.
Crabby took the box, and then
she found her keys to drive away.
She heard no clucking noise. The hen,
for once, had nothing more to say.

Crabby started up the truck.
She thought she heard a strangled cluck.
The rearview mirror showed the sight:
The hungry fox about to bite
the throat of Crabby's struggling hen
and drag her off into his den!

What could Crabby Cratchitt do?
If you were Crabby, what would *you*?

Crabby didn't make a sound.
She simply wheeled that truck around.
She drove it fast! She drove it hard!
She drove into the chicken yard.
She honked the horn. The fox turned gray.

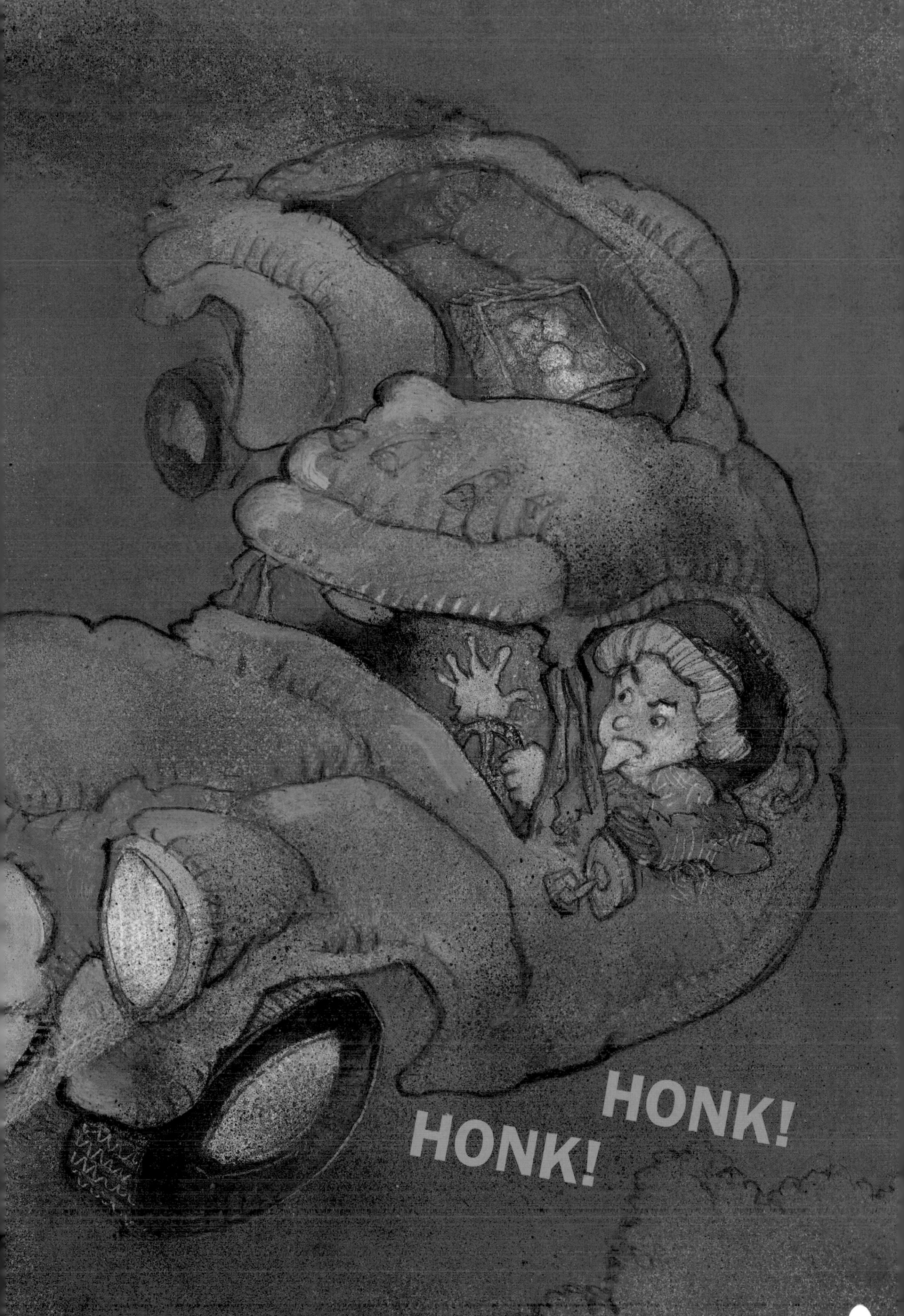
HONK!
HONK!

He dropped the hen and ran away.

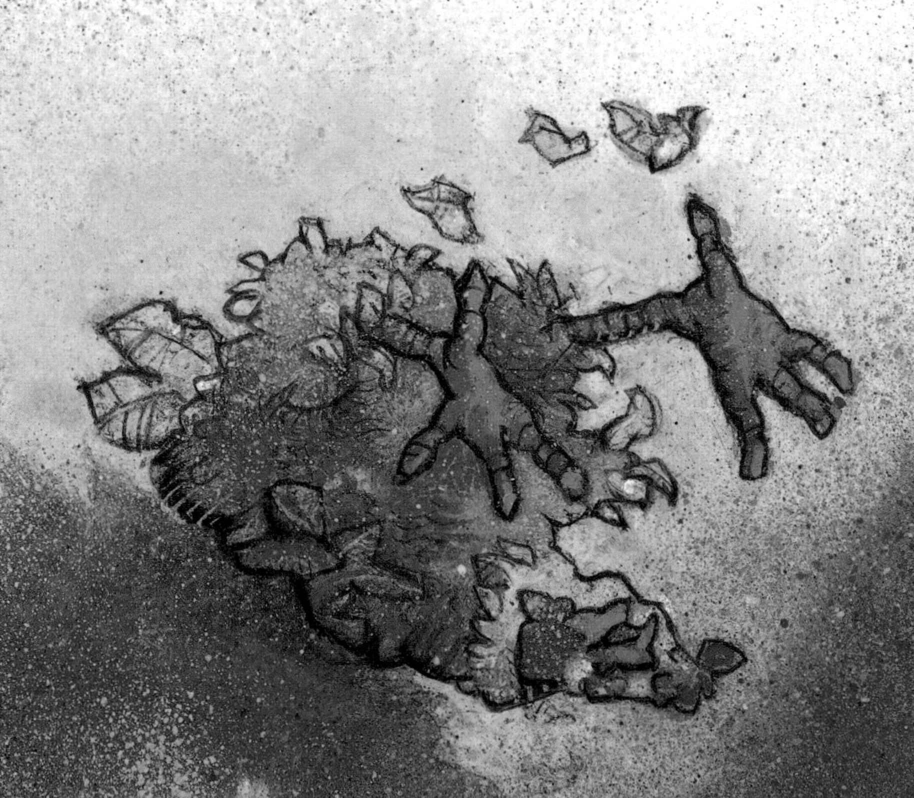

Crabby now could not deny it.
She'd never wanted *this* much quiet.
Crabby bounded from her truck.
The hen seemed lifeless, out of luck.
Crabby Cratchitt pleaded, "Cluck?"
"Cluck?" she said again. "*Please* cluck?"
The hen held still. The hen looked ill.
Crabby Cratchitt clucked until
she thought she heard a gasp of breath,
as if the hen had sidestepped death.

"Cluck!" said Crabby. "Let me hear it!"
The hen looked up with sudden spirit.
"Cluck!" cried Crabby. "Cluck with pride!"
"Cluck," the grateful hen replied.

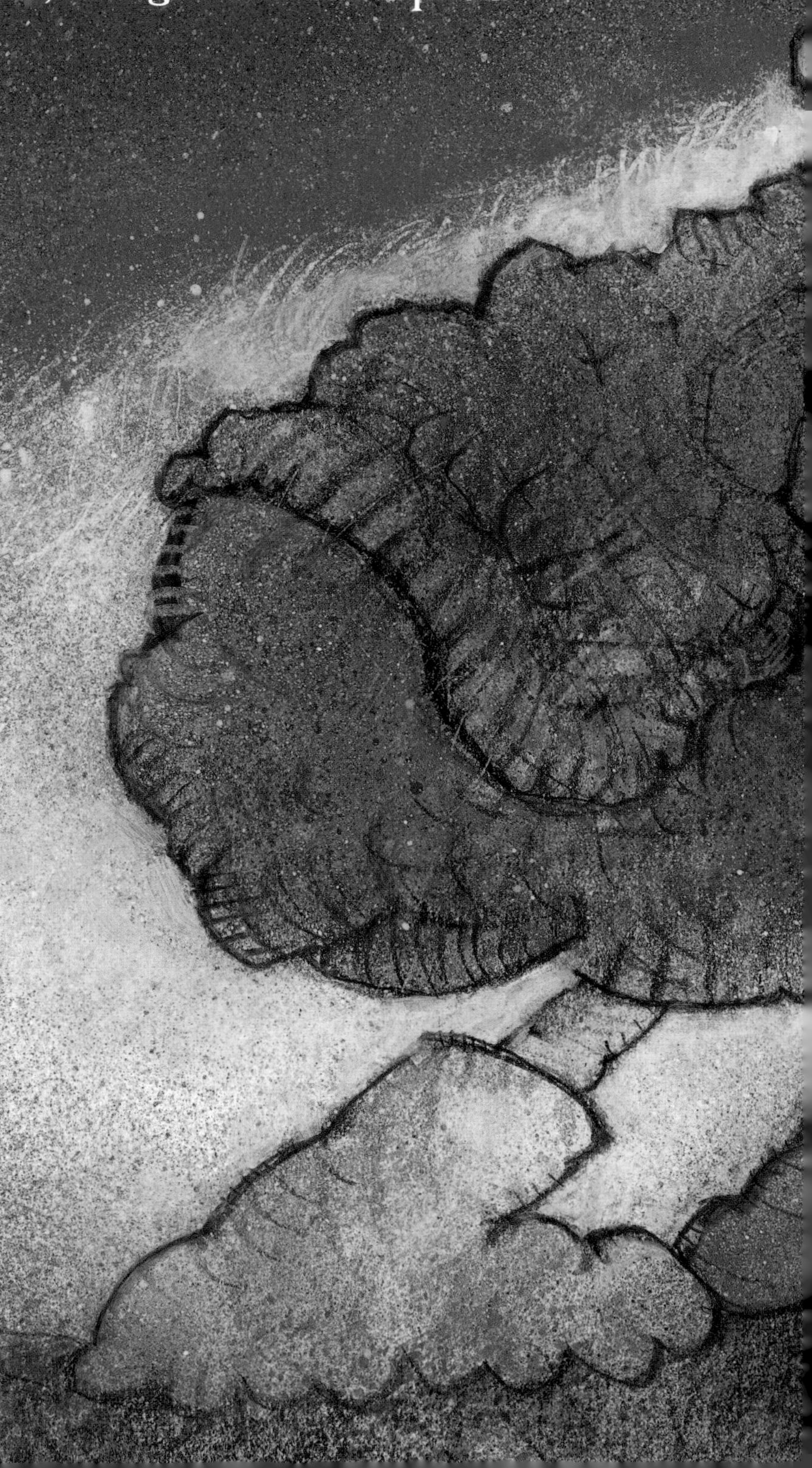

cluck

So that's the tale of Crabby Cratchitt,
E-I-E-I-oh.
An egg is best if you can hatch it,
E-I-E-I-oh.
The hen has chicks, and Crabby's proud!
They're fluffy, cute, and *very* loud.
Crabby likes the chicken choir.
She keeps them safe with chicken wire.
She listens to them all day long,
twenty peeping voices strong.

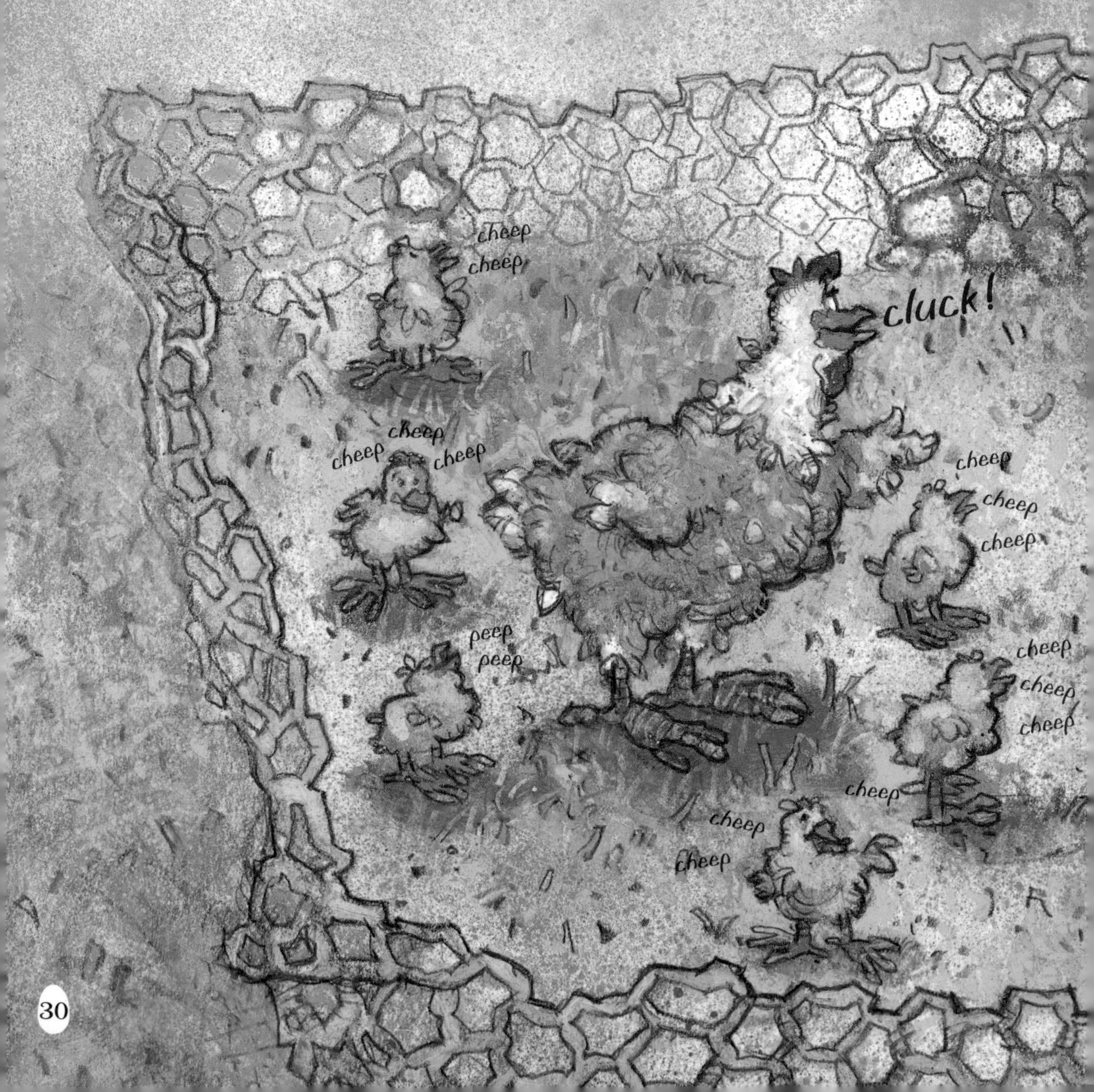

cheep
cheep
cheep
cheep
cheep
cheep
cheep
cheep
cheep
cheep
cheep
cheep
cheep
peep
cheep
peep
cheep
cheep
cheep
burp
cheep
cheep

At naptime, Crabby shuts her eyes.
She doesn't mind their lullabies.
She cannot hear a single cheep.
E-I-E-I . . . She's asleep!

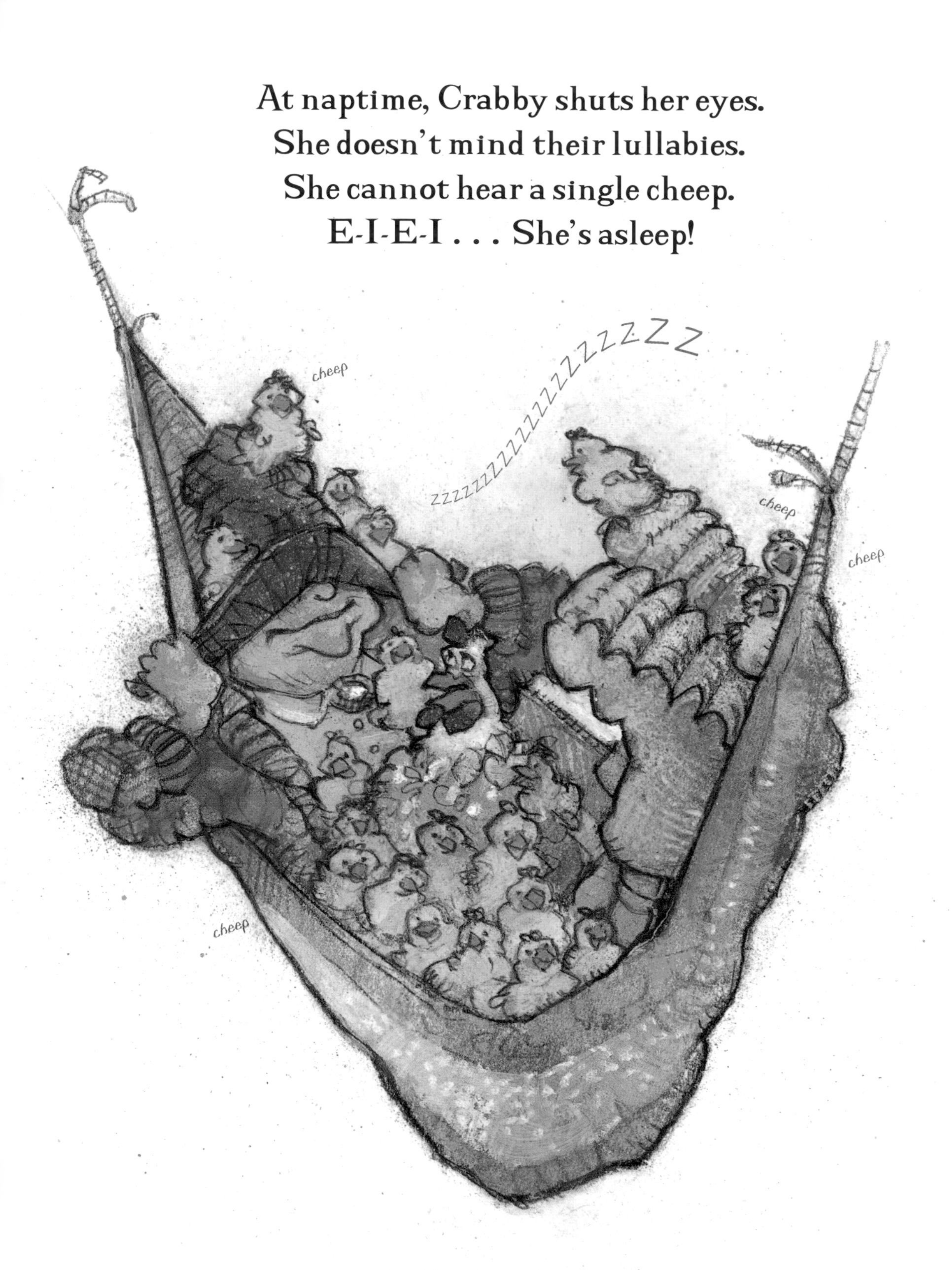

THE END